TEN SLY PIRANHAS

WILLIAM WISE

TEN SLY PIRANHAS

A Counting Story in Reverse
(A Tale of Wickedness—and Worse!)

pictures by VICTORIA CHESS

Dial Books for Young Readers 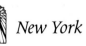 *New York*

Published by Dial Books for Young Readers
A Division of Penguin Books USA Inc.
375 Hudson Street · New York, New York 10014

Text copyright © 1993 by William Wise
Pictures copyright © 1993 by Victoria Chess
Design by Sara Reynolds
Printed in Hong Kong by
South China Printing Company (1988) Limited
First Edition
1 3 5 7 9 10 8 6 4 2

Library of Congress Cataloging in Publication Data

Wise, William, 1923–
Ten sly piranhas: a counting story in reverse, a tale
of wickedness—and worse!
by William Wise; pictures by Victoria Chess.
p. cm.
Summary: A school of ten sly piranhas gradually dwindles
as they waylay and eat each other.
ISBN 0-8037-1200-6 (trade).—ISBN 0-8037-1201-4 (library)
[1. Piranhas—Fiction. 2. Counting. 3 Stories in rhyme.]
I. Chess, Victoria, ill. II. Title.
PZ8.3.W743 1993 [E]—dc20 91-33704 CIP AC

For Jack and Eleanor,
who have lived among the real piranhas   w. w.

To Coco and Kyra with much love   v. c.

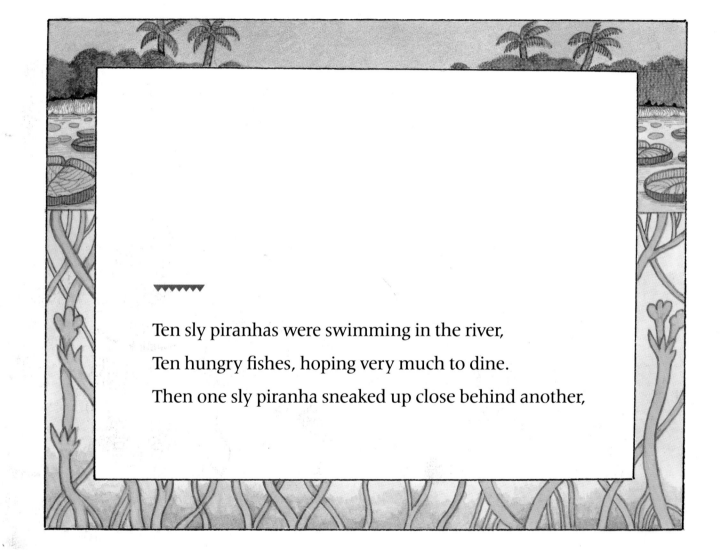

Ten sly piranhas were swimming in the river,

Ten hungry fishes, hoping very much to dine.

Then one sly piranha sneaked up close behind another,

And with a gulp, and a gurgle—
there were only nine.

▼▼▼▼▼▼

Nine sly piranhas were swimming in the river,

Nine little tricksters, who were lying there in wait.

Then one said, "My dear, you can trust me like a brother!"

And with a gulp, and a gurgle—
there were only eight.

▼▼▼▼▼▼

Eight sly piranhas were swimming in the river,

Frolicsome and frisky, and yet greatly to be feared.

Then all began to play a game of follow-the-leader,

And with a gulp, and a gurgle—
number eight had disappeared.

vvvvvv

Seven sly piranhas were swimming in the river,
Each a slippery schemer, with a dozen dirty tricks.
Then one said, "Come close, if you want
    to hear a secret!"

And with a gulp, and a gurgle—

there were only six.

▼▼▼▼▼▼

Six sly piranhas were swimming in the river,

Dreaming of their dinners, as piranhas often do.

Then one stopped to stare at some turtles

   that were passing,

And with a gulp, and a gurgle—
number six had vanished too.

vvvvvv

Five sly piranhas were swimming in the river,

Five roguish rascals, all rotten to the core.

Then one spied another, eating beetles at the bottom,

And with a gulp, and a gurgle—
there were only four.

▼▼▼▼▼▼

Four sly piranhas were swimming in the river,
Four cool connivers, each as crafty as could be.
Then one found a cave, and asked,
   "Shall we go exploring?"

And with a gulp, and a gurgle—
there were only three.

▼▼▼▼▼▼

Three sly piranhas were swimming in the river,
The last remaining members of that memorable crew.
Then one saw his neighbor growing sleepy
  in the sunlight,

And with a gulp, and a gurgle—
there were only two.

vvvvvv

Two sly piranhas were swimming in the river,
A pair of artful actors, just pretending to have fun.
Then the first cried, "Look out!
   There's a giant snake behind you!"

And with a gulp, and a gurgle—

there was only one.

▾▾▾▾▾▾

A single sly piranha was swimming in the river,

More cunning than the others,

for he'd vanquished every one.

Thought he'd grown so clever,

he could eat up *any*body,

But S N A P ! went Old Croc—

and then there were none.

No sly piranhas were swimming in the river,

Where not so long ago there'd been eight—nine—ten.

And so ends the story of those foxy little fishes—

Unless you'd like to hear it told the same way again.

A NOTE ABOUT PIRANHAS

Piranhas, also known as caribes, have iridescent scales and can grow up to a foot in length. They travel in tight schools in South American rivers, notably the Amazon. With their powerful jaws and razor-sharp triangular teeth, piranhas can attack cattle and people, though they usually eat other fish instead. And on occasion—"with a gulp, and a gurgle"—they do indeed feed on one another.